This Little Tiger
book belongs to:

_____

_____

_____

STAFFORDSHIRE LIBRARIES

3 8014 09061 5342

STAFFORDSHIRE LIBRARIES
ARTS AND ARCHIVES

3 8014 09061 534 2	
PET	22-Sep-2008
CF	£7.99
CANN	

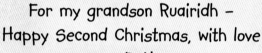

For my grandson Ruairidh –
Happy Second Christmas, with love
– D H

For Jim (Big Mouse) and Raechele (Little Mouse)
– J C

LITTLE TIGER PRESS
An imprint of Magi Publications
1 The Coda Centre, 189 Munster Road, London SW6 6AW
www.littletigerpress.com

First published in Great Britain 2005
This edition published 2008

Text copyright © Diana Hendry 2005
Illustrations copyright © Jane Chapman 2005
Diana Hendry and Jane Chapman have asserted their rights to be identified as the author
and illustrator of this work under the Copyright, Designs and Patents Act, 1988

A CIP catalogue record for this book is available from the British Library

All rights reserved • ISBN 978-1-84506-708-3
Printed in China
2 4 6 8 10 9 7 5 3 1

The Very Snowy Christmas

Diana Hendry

Jane Chapman

LITTLE TIGER PRESS

London

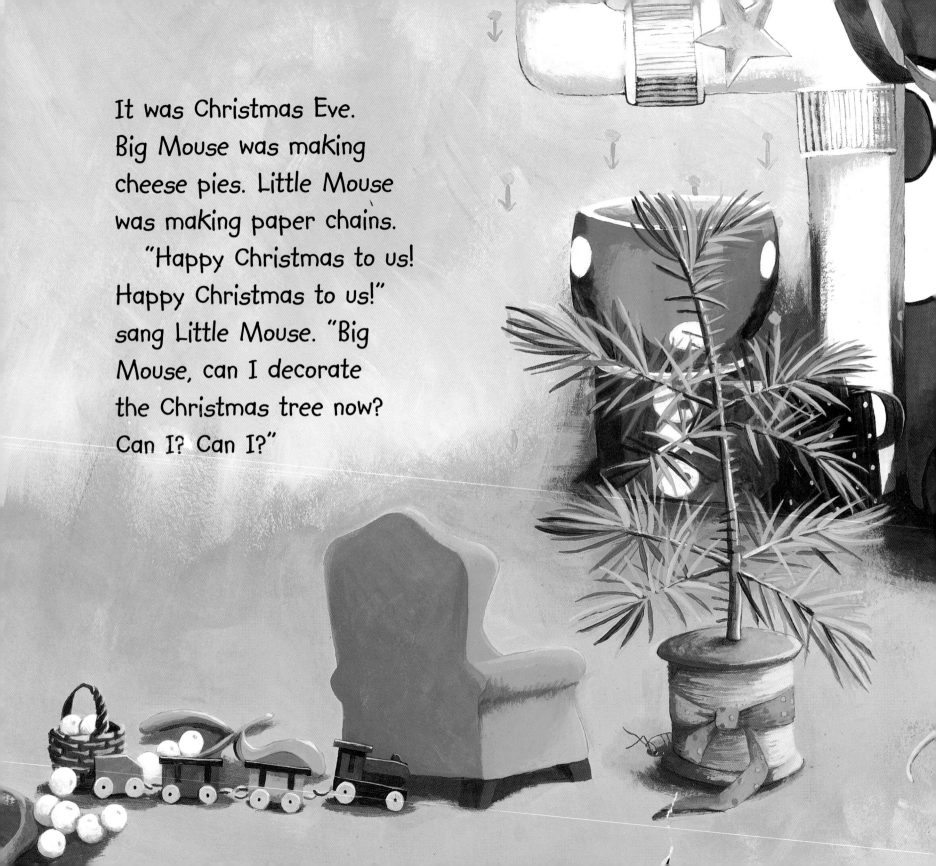

It was Christmas Eve.
Big Mouse was making
cheese pies. Little Mouse
was making paper chains.
   "Happy Christmas to us!
Happy Christmas to us!"
sang Little Mouse. "Big
Mouse, can I decorate
the Christmas tree now?
Can I? Can I?"

"We'll do it together," said Big Mouse.
Little Mouse hung golden acorns and
mistletoe berries on the tree.
Big Mouse put a star on the top.
"But we've forgotten the holly!"
cried Little Mouse. "I'll go and get
some." And off he rushed.
"Mind it has nice red berries!"
called Big Mouse.

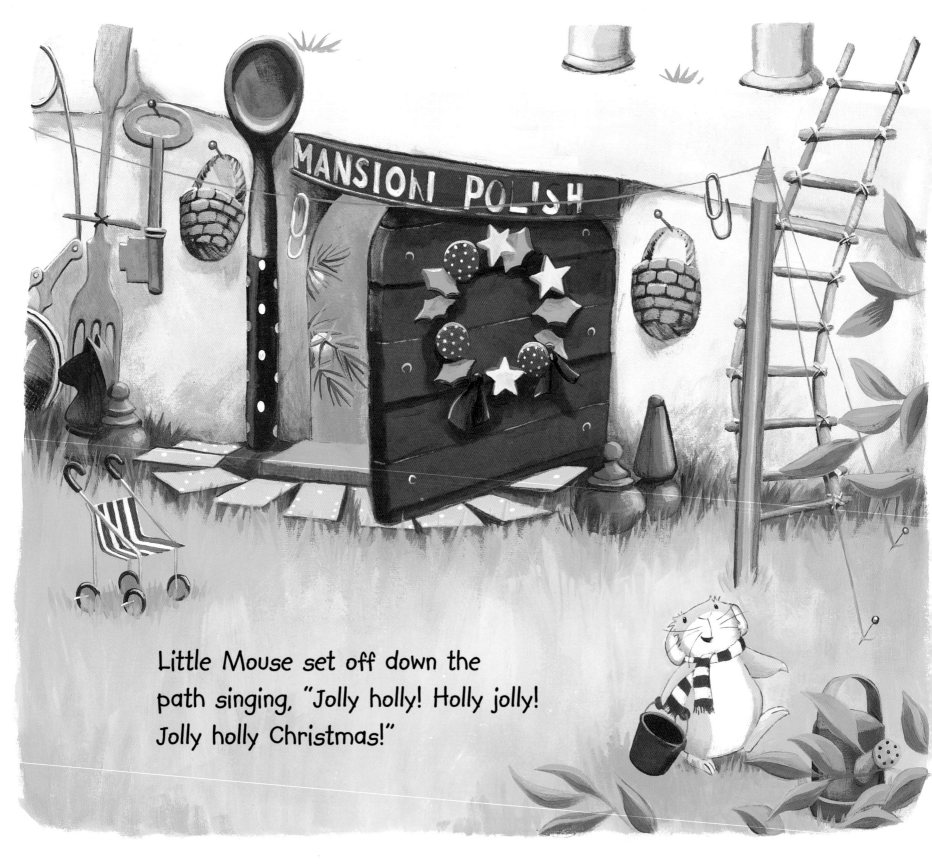

MANSION POLISH

Little Mouse set off down the
path singing, "Jolly holly! Holly jolly!
Jolly holly Christmas!"

But there was no holly to
be seen on the first corner.

And no holly on
the second corner.

And no holly on
the third corner.

Over the bridge ran
Little Mouse and at last
he found a holly bush with
shiny red berries. He jumped
up and down with excitement.

"Oh jolly holly! Holly jolly!
Jolly holly Christmas!" sang
Little Mouse, stretching high
on his toes to reach some.

But suddenly soft white flakes started falling all round him. One flake fell on Little Mouse's nose and made him sneeze. "Goodness me!" said Little Mouse. "The sky is coming undone!"

Little Mouse began to hurry home. Lots more pieces of sky were falling on him. Faster and faster they fell. They fell on his ears and his whiskers and his tail. "Oh dear, oh dear," said Little Mouse, "I'd better take some of this to show Big Mouse. He'll know how to stitch the sky together again."

Little Mouse made a ball of white flakes and put it in his bucket. Back over the bridge he hurried.

Suddenly he saw a strange creature
in the water, making faces at him.
It had lots of ears and a squiffy face,
and it waved its arms at Little Mouse.

"Ooooh!" squeaked Little Mouse.
"It's a Mouse Ness Monster!"
and he fell on his bottom.

"Oh, I wish Big Mouse was here!"
he cried, scrambling up.

Back down the path ran Little Mouse,
looking over his shoulder to see if the
Mouse Ness Monster was following
him. It wasn't, but something was!
Little Mouse could see its paw prints
coming after him.

"EEEEKkk! HELP! EEEEKkk!"
squeaked Little Mouse. "Now there's
an Invisible Monster chasing me!"

Little Mouse ran up
and down and round and
round in circles to escape,
but the paw prints of the Invisible
Monster went up and down and
round and round after him.

Little Mouse ran and ran.
Faster and faster whirled
the white flakes and faster
and faster ran Little Mouse.
And still the Invisible Monster
followed him.

At last Little Mouse saw his
house. But there in the garden
was a huge White Mouse!
"Oh no, no, no!" squeaked Little
Mouse. "Another monster
waiting to catch me!"
Little Mouse trembled
and began to cry.

But then the front door
opened and there was
Big Mouse. Little
Mouse leapt into
Big Mouse's arms.

"Big Mouse, Big Mouse," he cried,
"the sky has come undone! And look!"
he wailed, pointing to the paw
prints. "An Invisible Monster has
been following me, and there was
a terrible Mouse Ness Monster
in the water, and now that scary
White Mouse is staring at me!"

"Oh Little Mouse," said Big Mouse,
"the sky hasn't come undone.
It's SNOWING!

"And there aren't any
Invisible Monsters.
Those are your paw prints.

"And that Mouse Ness Monster
was your reflection in the water.
Look!" And Big Mouse showed
Little Mouse his face in a puddle.

"And this is a snow mouse I made to welcome you home," he said. "Let's make another." And so they did!

"Snow is magic!" cried Little Mouse.
"Yes," said Big Mouse. "Father Christmas likes snow too!"
Little Mouse jumped up and down. "Will he be here soon? Can I hang up my stocking now?"
"You can," said Big Mouse. "Let's go and get warm first."

So in they went and warmed their paws by the fire.

Little Mouse hung up his stocking and Big Mouse hung up his stocking too. The holly berries shone in the firelight.

"It's almost Christmas," said Little Mouse. "Jolly holly! Holly jolly! Jolly holly Christmas!" And he wriggled his warm toes.

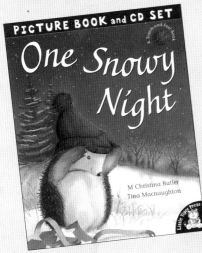

PICTURE BOOK and CD SET

One Snowy Night

M Christina Butler
Tina Macnaughton

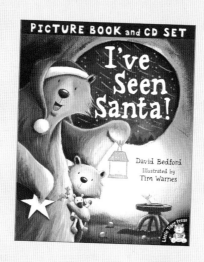

PICTURE BOOK and CD SET

I've Seen Santa!

David Bedford
Illustrated by
Tim Warnes

A Christmas Wish

JULIA HUBERY   SOPHY WILLIAMS

Perfect Christmas presents from Little Tiger Press

The Little Lost Robin

Elizabeth Baguley   Tina Macnaughton

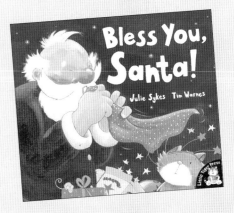

Bless You, Santa!

Julie Sykes   Tim Warnes

For information regarding any of the above titles
or for our catalogue, please contact us:
Little Tiger Press, 1 The Coda Centre,
189 Munster Road, London SW6 6AW
Tel: 020 7385 6333 Fax: 020 7385 7333
E-mail: info@littletiger.co.uk www.littletigerpress.com